Booger Jam

Miss Callahan's Booger Jam

By Tina Gabelein

Illustrated by Deon Matzen

MINDSTIR MEDIA

Dooger Jam
Copyright © 2015 Tina Gabelein. All rights reserved.

Illustrations by Deon Matzen

Published by Mindstir Media, LLC
1931 Woodbury Ave. #182 | Portsmouth, New Hampshire 03801 | USA
1.800.767.0531 | www.mindstirmedia.com

Printed in the United States of America
ISBN-13: 978-0-9969689-7-3
Library of Congress Control Number: 2015917626

Miss Callahan's preschool class was always exciting, and fun. There was playdough, painting, and coloring books. The children loved all the projects and centers where they got to play, but they especially loved circle time on Wednesday.

Show-and-tell was on
Wednesdays during
circle time. What a
great way to learn
about everyone and
see what kinds of
awesome things they
had. Once Erin
brought a real
robin's nest
that had fallen
from an apple tree in her backyard. It still
had some feathers and a blue eggshell in it.

Howie liked to bring something from his matchbox car collection. There must have been 100 cars in that collection!

Andy brought in a butterfly game
that everyone was able to play.

Jack brought in a snakeskin that
he found while camping with his
family. It was creepy, and the girls
were afraid to touch it.

Show-n-tell was always an adventure.
Whenever circle time came around, especiall
during show-n-tell,

the kids did one of their favorite things...
PICKING THIER NOSES!

This grossed Miss Callahan out! She would
have to interrupt show-n-tell constantly to tell
the children, "Please stop picking your noses!"

Being told that picking their nose was gross, and a great big NO No!

only made the children feel they needed to pick their noses EVEN MORE!

One day as the children sat at circle comfortably picking their noses, Miss Callahan stood up

and said, "ENOUGH! I have given everyon plenty of chances to stop all this nose pickin If you are all going to continue to pick, I w just have to make you...Booger Jam! Yes...tha is exactly what I'll do, and it will be absolute wonderful this time

"This time?" asked Erin. "You mean you've made Booger Jam before?" The children immediately stopped picking their noses and stared in wonder. Jack raised his hand and asked, "Miss Callahan, how can YOU make Booger Jam?"

"Well, it is quite easy actually, but first, I will have to collect large amounts of boogers. This should take no time at all." Then she laughed and said, "My recipe is a secret. I've had to make it once before. It was very good and everyone liked it on biscuits."

"EWW, GROSS, YUCK!" Whined the children, as they promised to never pick their noses again.

The children began bragging about how they would never have to eat Miss Callahan's Booger Jam, since they were never going to pick their noses again!

romise!

Days passed and soon the children forgot about the Booger Jam, and their promise to Miss Callahan.

Several weeks passed, and the children brought lots of great things for Show-n-Tell, a stick horse from Santa and a baby doll that cried real tears.

Howie finally brought something other than [
car collection. He brought a baby hedgehog!
Oh! and his mom too.

She held the hedgehog and everyone was allowed to touch this new pet. It looked prickly but was actually soft, and its pink little nose wiggled when the kids touched its back.

But...Something was happening. Can you guess what the kids were doing? Yep, you guessed it! The children were continuing to pick their noses.

Miss Callahan was so grossed out, but she did not remind the class anymore. She would just smile and think about the Booger Jam she would be making soon.

Then one special day, just as show-n-tell
was ending, Miss Callahan said, "I have
a surprise for you all!" She had a big
grin on her face, and she winked at the
kids. Everyone waited patiently
expecting something
wonderful.

The last time she brought a surprise for show-n-tell it was an ice-cream maker. The children took turns turning the crank, while they sang songs. It took a very long time, but the ice-cream was worth the wait. Her class decided that homemade ice-cream is the best ice-cream in the whole wide world!

The children waited patiently, quietly watching their teacher. Miss Callahan was calmer than usual, and no one saw anything that looked like the ice-cream maker.

Andy could not stand it any longer. The silence was driving him crazy and he yelled out, "What is it?" Then Miss Callahan brought out a box from under her desk. She slowly opened up the box and pulled out a glass jar.

Oh no! It's the Booger Jam. How did she do it? Where did she get all those boogers?" moaned Jack. The children looked at each other and gasped in horror. Howie and Erin slowly pulled their fingers from their noses.

"Yes," Said Miss Callahan. "it is Booger Jam. I made you Booger Jam! Just look at it, it turned out perfect."

There in her hand was the Booger Jam.

Miss Callahan's
Booger Jam

Shades of green with little black specks all gooey and swirled together in a glass jar. Could it possibly be a million boogers all cooked and jelled into one giant booger?

"Okay children," said Miss Callahan, "let's settle down now, after all it is snack time. Head over to your spots at the table and let us get out the crackers and juice. We may need to wash down the Booger Jam." "I thought we would have biscuits." Said Erin, disappointed.

"Oh dear," said Miss Callahan, "I'm sorry, I was visiting my cousin's farm all weekend, and didn't have enough time to make biscuits, since I was making jam. Crackers are just as good with Booger Jam, you'll see." Half-heartedly, everyone made their way over to the snack table. They dragged their feet, moaned and feared the Booger Jam.

Mrs. Calahan smiled and began to tell the children about her weekend. She told them of the fun she had hiking and picking berries on the farm, and of course, making the special jam. Jack tilted his head sideways and imagined berries, in the shape of noses with boogers, growing on bushes... he shuttered.

"Okay, come on everyone, at least try a little taste! You will be very surprised. It's better than you think." Said Miss Callahan.

Jack was known as the bravest boy in the whole class. They called him, "Jack the Fearless." He claimed to have hang-glided off Mt. Everest with his Uncle, and that he had chased down a pack of rabid dingos in the outback.

Jack thought, if I can eat this Booger Jam, my title of "Jack the Fearless" will prove that I really am fearless. So, Jack closed his eyes and took a tiny bite.

His face scrunched up. His eyes got big and he stuck out his tongue! Everyone gasped in horror!

Suddenly, Jack's eyes opened and he had a puzzled look on his face. "Well guys, it's not that bad..... I actually think it tastes GOOD! Hey everyone, try it!"

Said Jack.

Erin was next. Juice in hand, ready for an emergency wash down, she slowly dipped her index finger into the greenish glob on her cracker, and stuck it in her mouth.
"EEK ACK! she squawked.

"Hmm...." she said. "It's good! It looks horrible but it doesn't taste anything like boogers!"
Each of the children begain tasting the Booger Jam. With smiles, giggles and laughter all around the table everyone finally became brave enough to try the crackers and jam.

What a relief to find out that Booger Jam was yummy after all. "See, isn't it good?" aske Miss Callahan.

"I'll let you in on a littl secret. I've been eatin Booger Jam my whole life The children stared at thei teacher. "Don't worry it really has nothin to do with nose picking

My cousin has a far called Gooseberry Hi They grow lots and lots c gooseberries there. "Oh Said the children, st wondering about this mysterious jar

U-PICK GOOSEBERRIES

My Uncle lives on a farm and he as a goose, but I have never seen any berries growing on that old goose.

"No children, gooseberries grow on bushes. You have to pick the berries. Much like you children pick your noses and we are not going to have any more picking are we?" asked Miss Callahan. "No NEVER!" said the children. "Good! Is it a promise then?" she asked. "YES Miss Callahan!" her class replied. Thank you, I am so glad to hear this."

D-R-R-I-I-N-G!!! went the bell. "Phew, it's recess time!" Yelled Andy.

Miss Callahan's class had survived the Booger Jam. Everyone promised never to pick their noses again, but have the children learned their lesson, or will they forget and contine to pick? Time will tell!

Miss Callahan's Booger Jam
4 pints fresh gooseberries
7 cups sugar
2 Tbls. lemon juice
1 cup fruit pectin
prepared canning jars and canner
1 cup "secret" ingredient
Prep time: 10 minutes
Makes approx. 9 cups
Directions: add your freshly cleaned berries to a saucepan. Stir in the lemon juice, sugar, secret ingredient, and pectin. Continuously stirring bringing your ingredients to a boil for one full minute. Remove from heat. Skim off any foam that has formed. Quickly ladle the mixture into your prepared jars and process. ENJOY!

About the Author

I live on an old farm in the Pacific Northwest on beautiful Whidbey Island. I have been a preschool teacher for over twenty-five years, and enjoy the fresh energy and creativity teaching brings to my life. Everyday is a new beginning, with adventure and opportunity to inspire young hearts. My goals have always been to model good behavior, encourage "The Golden Rule," and keep education fun. Preschool teachers struggle daily with their students picking their noses. I for one, find this disgusting. It is a hard habit to break and most children do not realize they are doing it. I really wanted to find an impressionable way to teach my students to stop picking their noses. One evening as I was grocery shopping, I spied an interesting jar of jam on the shelf. It had an incredible resemblance to what I envisioned a collection of boogers would look like, and that is where my story of Booger Jam began.

Special thanks to:
My grandkids, Jack and Erin, who always love to hear their Pinky's crazy stories and adventures, Deon Matzen who made Booger Jam come to life with her imagery, and to my ever patient family, who continually puts up with all my zaniness on a regular basis, I love you all!

About the Illustrator

Deon Matzen resides on Whidbey as well and has illustrated other children's books including *Chipper, the Heroic Chipmunk*, and *Friendly Feathers*. She is an award winning artist and educator having taught at the local community college and is now helping retirees repurpose their lives through painting. Her paintings have been featured in SouthwestArt Magazine, American Art Collector, Readers' Digest Book of Drawing and international Artist's book, How did you Paint That?. You can view her work on her website www.theruralgallery.com and keep up with her latest activities on her facebook page www.facebook/DeonMatzenArtist.

Working with Tina has been a joy even if drawing children with their didgits up their noses is not my chosen topic. We had a lot of laughs over this one.

CPSIA information can be obtained at www.ICGtesting.com
Printed in the USA
LVIW01n0500200216
475930LV00004B/9